"Cut & Tell"

Scissor Stories for Fall

by

Jean Warren

Totline Press
Warren Publishing House
P.O. Box 2255, Everett, WA 98203

original paper plate cut-outs

and

stories

by

Jean Warren

taken from back issues

of the

Totline Newsletter

DOLSON HILL LIBRARY
PIPESTONE, MINNESOTA

ACKNOWLEDGEMENTS

Dedicated to David Van Warren, my #1 son.

Copyright © 1984 Jean Warren

All rights reserved, except for the inclusion of brief quotations in a review or for classroom use, no part of this book may be reproduced in any form without the written permission of the publisher.

ISBN 0-911019-03-0

Library of Congress Catalogue Card Number 84-051352

Cover design and story pictures by Larry Countryman, Snohomish, WA

Graphic direction and patterns by Jeff McBride, Seattle, WA

Manufactured in the United States of America.

Published by Warren Publishing House, P.O. Box 2255, Everett, WA 98203

Distributed by Gryphon House, Inc.
P.O. Box 275
Mt. Rainier, MD 20712

PREFACE

For years, my family has rotated between thinking I was crazy and knowing I was crazy. For who but a disturbed person would spend all day cutting up paper plates. The fact that I enjoyed it was negated by the dishes that piled up, the beds that were left unmade and the piles of scrap plates in the living room.

But alas, there now seems to have been a reason to my madness. Stories and cut-outs to delight young children and a process to intrigue adults. Who knows, you may catch the madness and never look at a paper plate the same way again.

Seriously, the art (if I may be permitted to use this term) of paper plate cutting is fun and challenging. Many people ask how I come up with the cut-outs for my stories. Actually, I must confess, I do them backwards. First, I come up with a possible cut-out and then I write a story to fit.

Once, I was trying to come up with a paper plate crab. After a few attempts, I decided to give up on the crab because I was getting no-where. In fact, the cut-outs were beginning to resemble a frog. So I decided to try to make a frog. Twenty or more paper plates later, I finally had to admit the frog wasn't coming either — but it did vaguely resemble a spider. So why not? I'll go for a spider. Piles of plates later, when I was ready to admit that no way was I ever going to make a good spider, I looked down at my paper plate and there to my surprise was my crab!

I haven't quite figured out the creative process, but I do know you have to be free. You have to be willing to experiment and follow your instincts and be willing to go on to something new if the old doesn't work.

CONTENTS

CONTENTS

HELPFUL HINTS

STORY TELLING

Some cut-outs will stand up on their own, but others will need to be propped up to be seen. A small felt board or blackboard tray would work well.

It is also a good idea to practice cutting the cut-outs and reading the story several times before presenting the story to young children. He who hesitates and/or is unsure what to do next may lose many young listeners.

CUTTING PATTERNS

The intention of the "Cut & Tell" stories is that the story teller would mark a paper plate with cutting lines and then cut sections of the plate as they tell the story.

It is, however, not absolutely necessary to cut out the paper plate objects while reading the story. If the story teller prefers, he/she may pre-cut the plate and merely hold up the appropriate section as they reach a certain part in the story.

Pre-cut sections should be hidden from children until the appropriate time in the story to heighten the story's surprise.

HELPFUL HINTS

ADDING FEATURES

Most paper objects are fine just as they are cut out. Animals cut-outs, however, may need eyes or markings. Eyes can be made quickly with a hole punch or you can draw them on with a black marking pen.

USING THE PATTERNS

Cut-out patterns are given in two forms.

* ½ of a regular-sized paper plate with cutting lines
* A full-sized smaller circle with cutting lines, which teachers can use to make copies for themselves or their children.

The wavy edge of a real paper plate adds to the character of the cut-outs, however, plain paper is often easier to use with large groups of children. The heavier the paper used, the sturdier will be the cut-outs.

Permission is granted from Warren Publishing House for teachers to make copies of the cut-out patterns to use with students.

USING THE STORIES WITH CHILDREN

PRESCHOOL CHILDREN

Young children love hearing the story repeated again and again as you re-cut additional paper plates. Take advantage of this repetition and begin letting the children finish parts of the story or tell what is going to happen next.

After children have heard the story many times, ask them to tell you step-by-step, what happens next in the story.

Make a cut-out for each of your children and let them paint or color the cut-out as a follow-up activity.

Preschool children would also enjoy using the non-three dimensional cut-outs as circle puzzles. Give them the cut-out pieces and let them figure out how it all goes back together into a circle shape. Cut-out stories that would make good puzzles are: The Apple Tree, Three Brave Hunters, Two Friendly Ghosts and The Wise Old Owl.

USING THE STORIES WITH CHILDREN

KINDERGARTEN CHILDREN

If you are working with kindergarten children you can do all of the above mentioned activities, plus more advanced ones. Kindergarten children should be able to retell the story more completely on their own. In fact, they should be able to retell the story to you as you re-cut another paper plate.

Kindergarten children should also be able to decorate their own cut-outs more elaborately. Many of them may be able to cut out their own paper plates, as the teacher re-reads the story.

FIRST AND SECOND GRADE CHILDREN

First and second grade children should be able to cut out their own cut-outs and decorate them.

They can also write or read the story on their own if the teacher would re-write it on a large story chart or run off mimeographed copies of the story for each child.

THE APPLE TREE

THE APPLE TREE

Adapted from the Traditional American Fingerplay

(1) (2)

Way up high in an apple tree,
Small white blossoms, I could see.
I watered that tree and what do you know!
Little green apples began to grow.

(3) (4)

Way up high in an apple tree,
Two red apples smiled at me.
I shook that tree as hard as I could. **(5)**
Down came those apples,
MMMMM, they were good!

CUTTING DIRECTIONS

(1) Fold paper plate in half and cut as indicated.

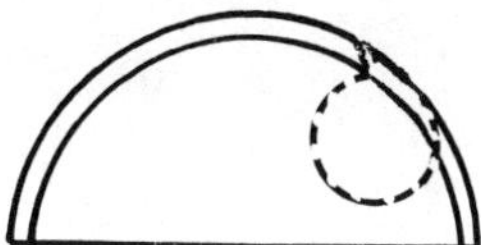

(2) Remove the two cut sections and hold up your tree.

(3) Fold the tree back together and fold the outer branches over, towards the center fold, creating another fold. Cut as shown on this fold, creating two pointed cuts when the tree is opened.

(4) Place the two circles in the slits and continue the story.

(5) Shake your tree and let your apples fall out.

EXTENDED ACTIVITIES

Counting

Divide apples in half or fourths. Let your children decide how many apples will be needed for everyone to receive a piece.

When you cut open an apple, let your children count out how many seeds are inside.

Feeling

Place three different fruits in a "feelie" bag. Let your children touch each fruit and find the apple by identifying its characteristics.

Smelling

Cut open three fruits and have your children identify each with their eyes closed by smelling.

Apple Surprise

Help your children cut an apple in half sideways. Look for the surprise star inside.

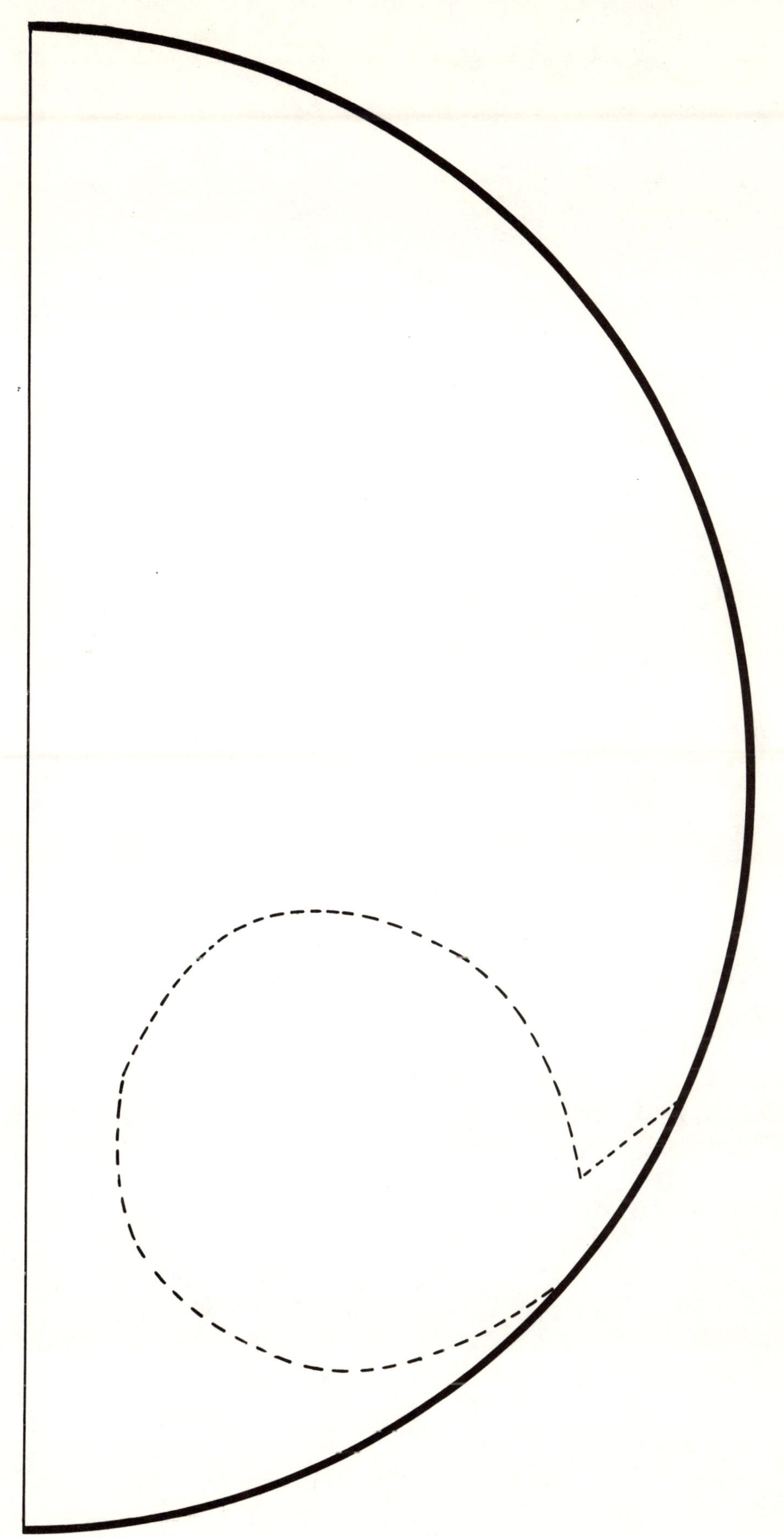

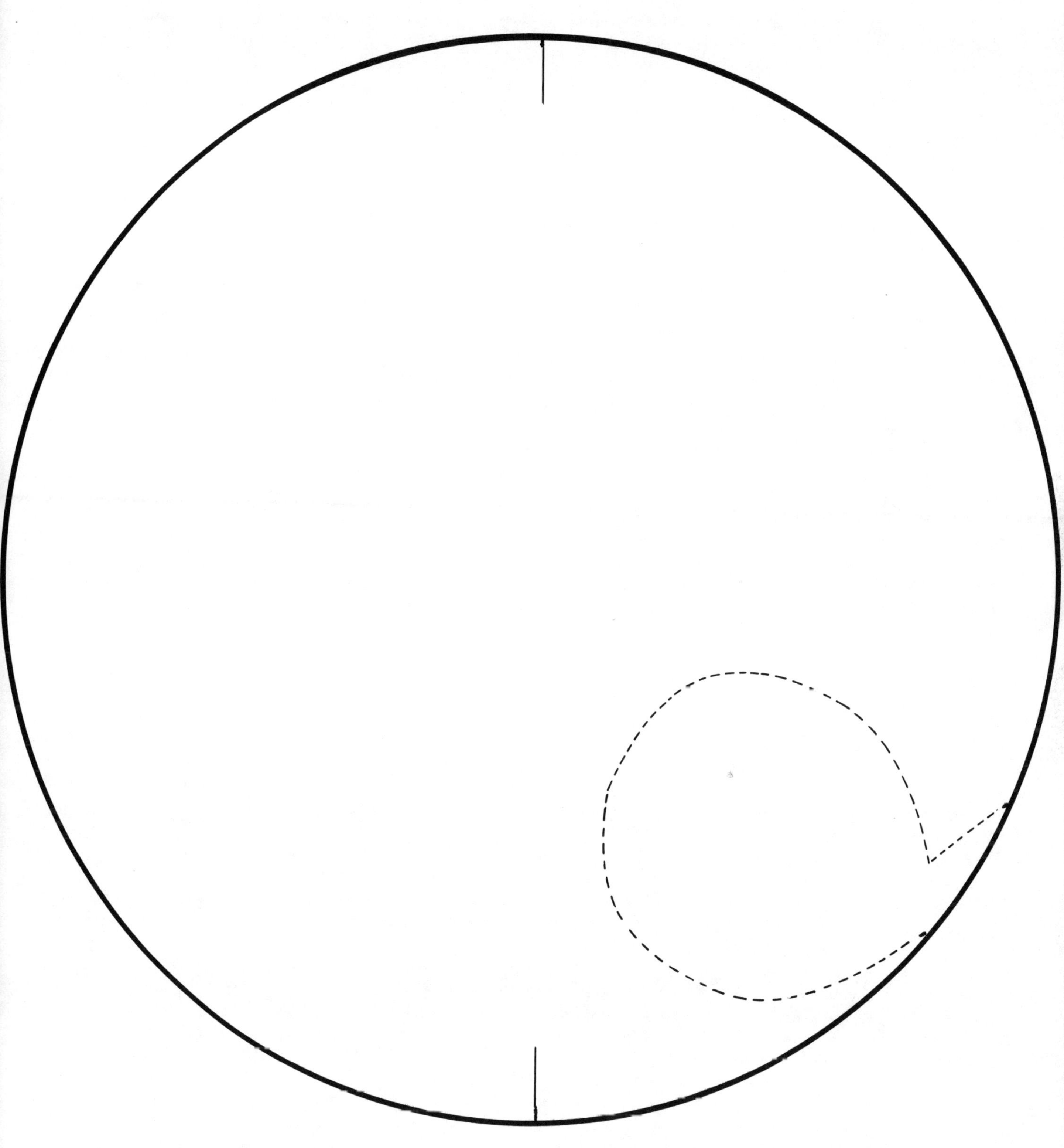

DANNY AND THE WOODEN DUCK

DANNY AND THE WOODEN DUCK

Danny loved ducks. He wished he could have a real duck but ducks needed to be free and live in open spaces and Danny lived in a tall apartment building in a large city. **(1) (2) (3)**

Danny's grandfather knew he loved ducks, so he carved him a beautiful wooden duck for his birthday. **(4) (5)**

Danny loved his wooden duck but somehow it wasn't quite the same as a real duck.

One day, Danny was playing with his wooden duck and he wished his duck had soft feathers just like real ducks. And do you know what? Danny's duck grew real feathers all over his body. Danny stroked the soft duck feathers but he wasn't happy. He wished his duck could walk and talk like a real duck. And do you know what? Danny's duck started waddling all around Danny's room quacking. Danny loved watching and listening to his duck but he still wasn't happy. He wanted his duck to be real.

Danny wished his duck could swim. And do you know what? When Danny placed his wooden duck in the bathtub, it started swimming around and around. Danny loved watching his duck swim around but he still wasn't happy. Danny wanted his duck to be just like a real duck. If only his duck could fly. Danny wished and wished his duck could fly. And do you know what? Danny's duck started flying around his room. Danny loved watching his wooden duck fly around his room but Danny still wasn't happy. He wanted his duck to be like a real duck.

Then Danny remembered. Real ducks need to be free and live in open spaces. Danny wished with all his heart that his little duck could be real — so he opened his window and let his duck be free. And do you know what? Danny's duck flew straight out the window and joined a group of ducks flying south. **(6)**

Danny wasn't sad to see his duck fly away. Danny was happy because his duck was real at last!

CUTTING DIRECTIONS

(1) Cut out pattern.

(2) Open duck body out flat.

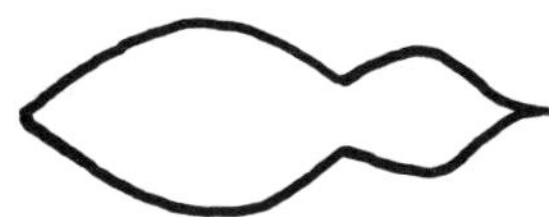

(3) Fold the duck's body (1 & 3/4" below the head. Make a 1" cut from the fold on the center line — leaving a 2" slit when opened.)

(4) Cut wings apart.

(5) Stick the wings down through the center slit about 1". Fold out the bottom of the wing section for feet. Hold the duck in the center of its body to keep it from falling apart.

(6) Raise your arm up and down and the duck will appear to fly.

EXTENDED ACTIVITIES

Signs of Fall

Encourage your children to notice signs of fall. Much will depend on where you live but some general ones include:

People:

Buy or make warm clothes
Buy or chop wood
Rake leaves

Animals:

Store food
Grow warmer fur
Hibernate
Fly south

Plants:

Change the color of their leaves
Leaves fall to the ground
Foods ripen and are harvested
Flowers die and drop seeds

Surroundings:

The soil gets harder
Daylight is shorter
The temperature gets cooler

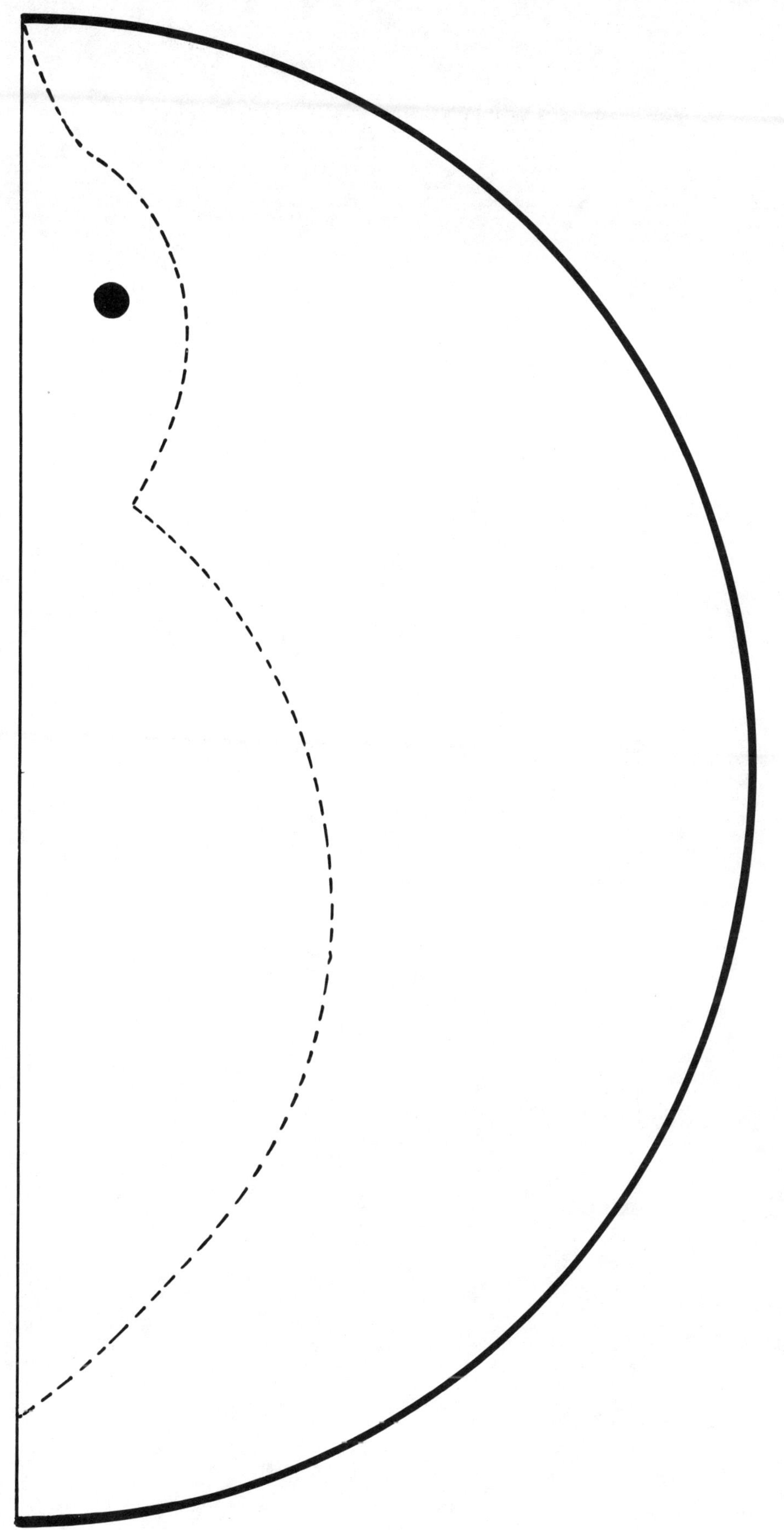

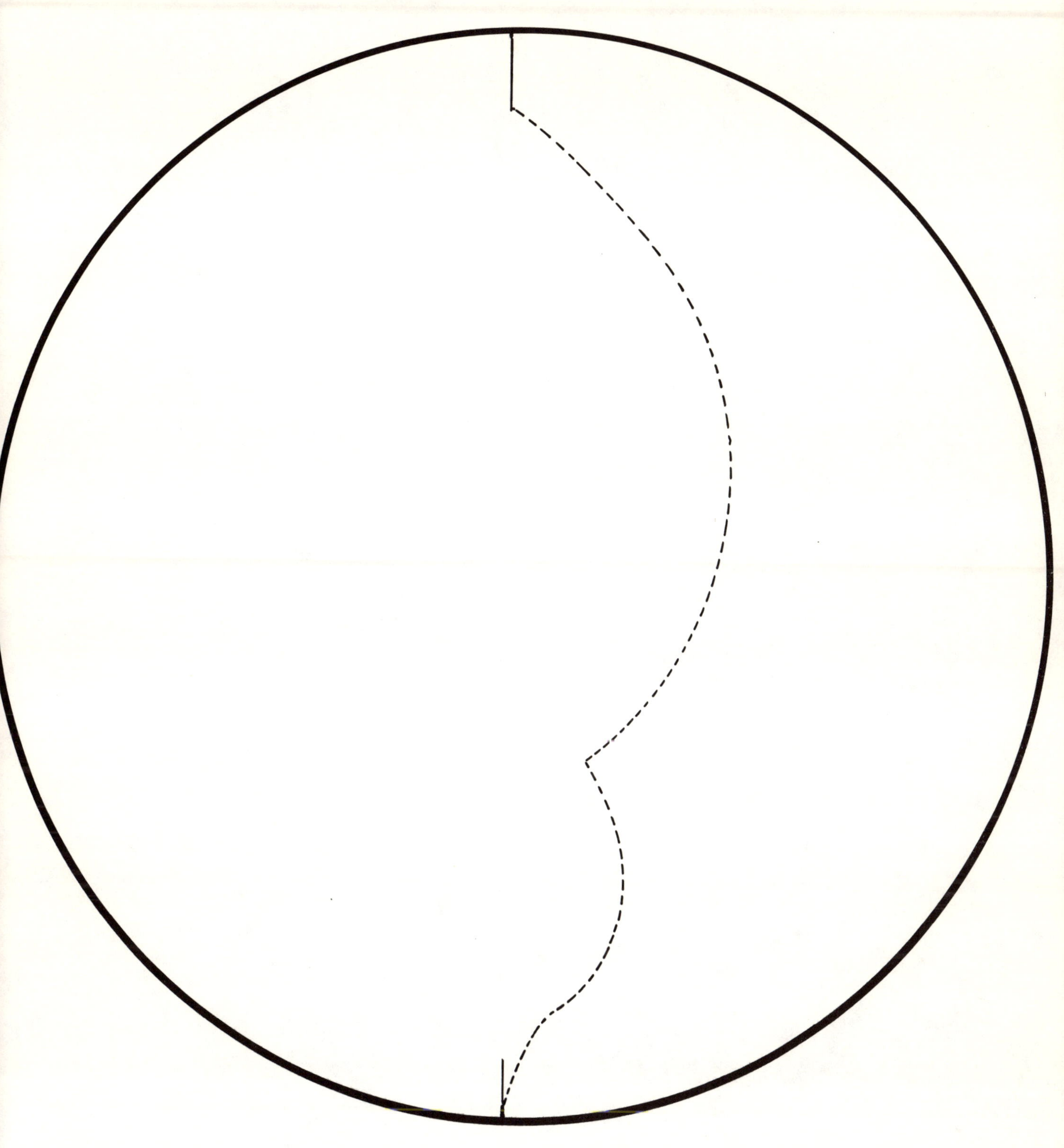

FOUR AUTUMN LEAVES

FOUR AUTUMN LEAVES

(1) (2) (3)

Four Autumn leaves
In a big old tree
One blew off
Then there were __________ . **(4)**

Three little leaves
With nothing to do
Another blew off
Then there were __________ .

Two little leaves
In the Autumn sun.
One blew off
Then there was __________ .

Being all alone
Wasn't much fun
The last one blew off
Then there were __________ .

Four little leaves
Beneath the big old tree
One blew away
Then there were __________ . **(5)**

Three little leaves
With nothing to do
Another blew away
Then there were __________ .

Two little leaves
In the Autumn sun.
One blew away
Then there was __________ .

Being all alone
Wasn't much fun
The last one blew away
And then there were __________ .

CUTTING DIRECTIONS

(1) Cut out leaves.

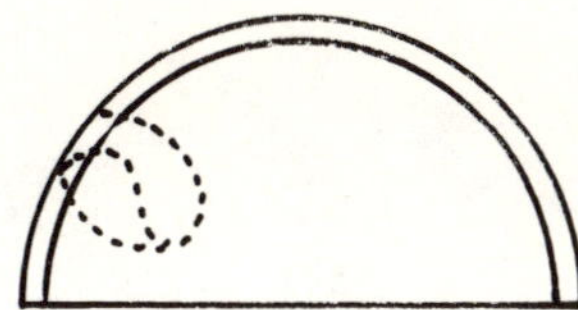

(2) Fold branches back half-way and cut slits as shown.

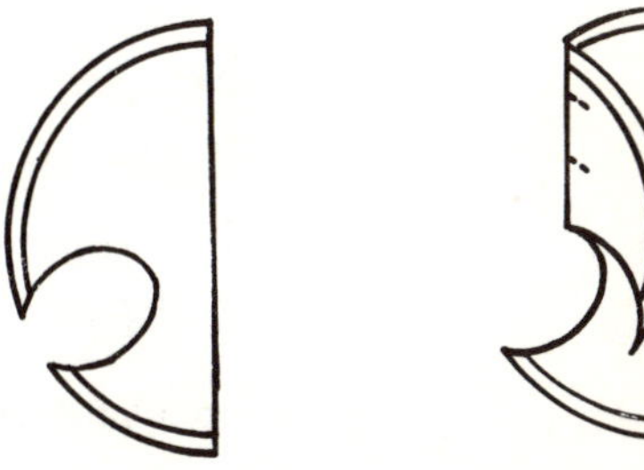

(3) Open tree and place leaves in slits.

(4) Remove leaves as the story indicates.

(5) Take leaves away one at a time.

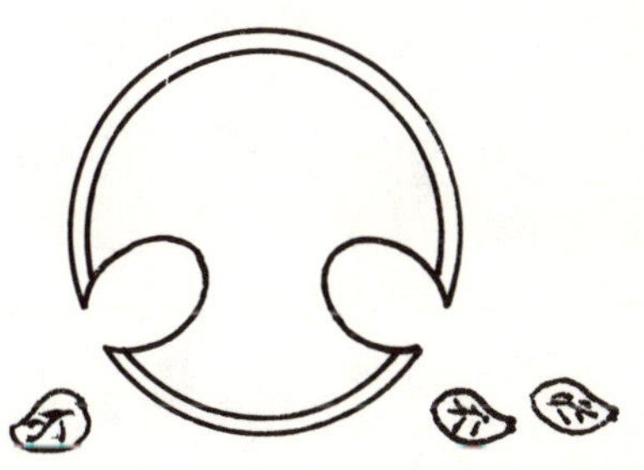

EXTENDED ACTIVITIES

Music

LEAVES

Sung to: "Twinkle, Twinkle Little Star"

All join hands and circle round
While we watch the leaves fall down.

See them twirling to the ground
See them whirling all around.

See them skipping here and there
See them flipping in the air.

Autumn leaves so peacefully
Falling, falling from the tree.

Dramatics

Have children pretend they are playing in the leaves. Have them rake the leaves, jump in the leaves, toss the leaves, roll in the leaves.

Another fun activity is to have your children pretend that they are the leaves falling off the tree. Have them think up different ways the leaves could fall from the tree. Examples: spinning, swaying, floating, falling slowly, etc.

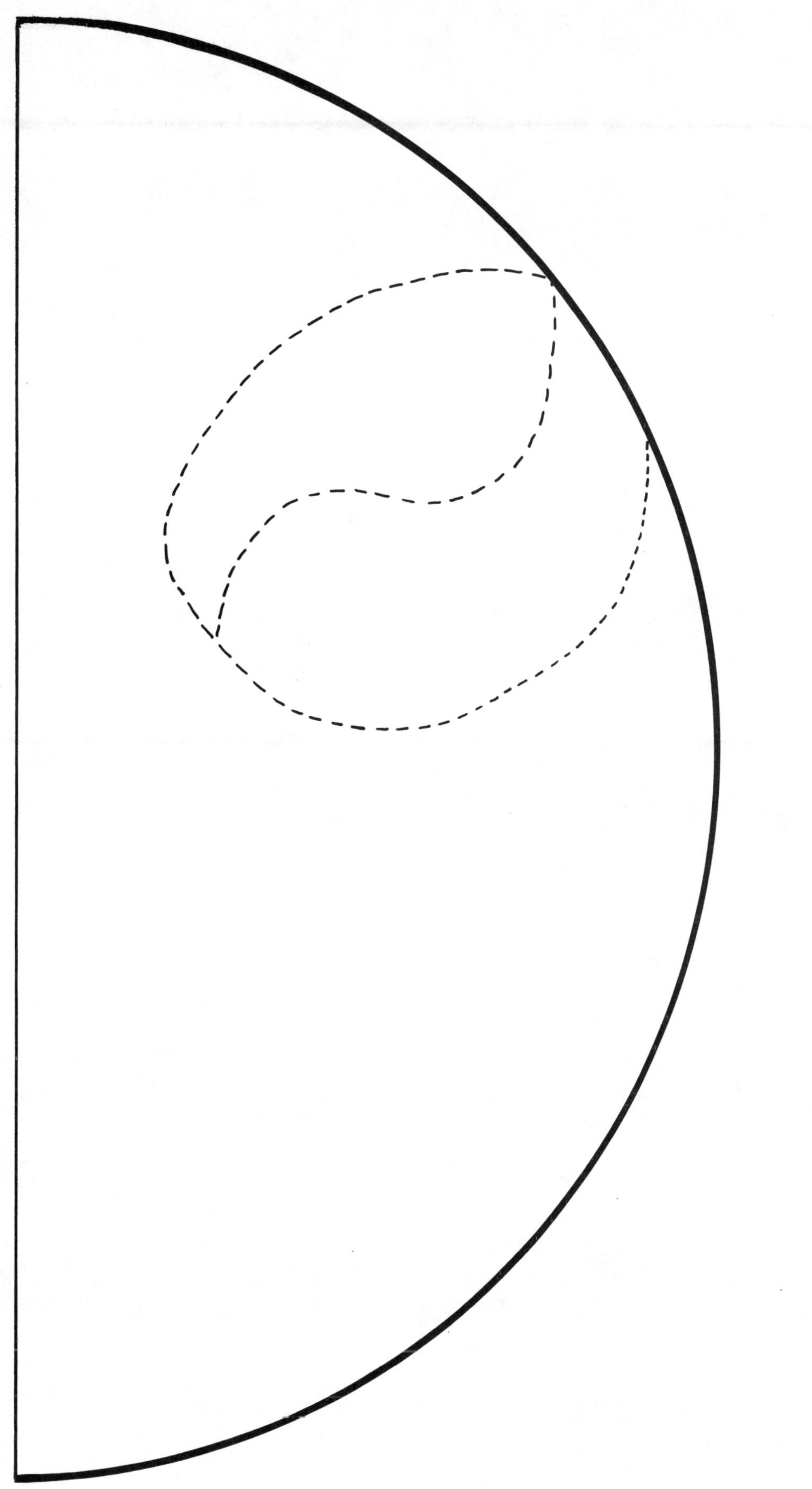

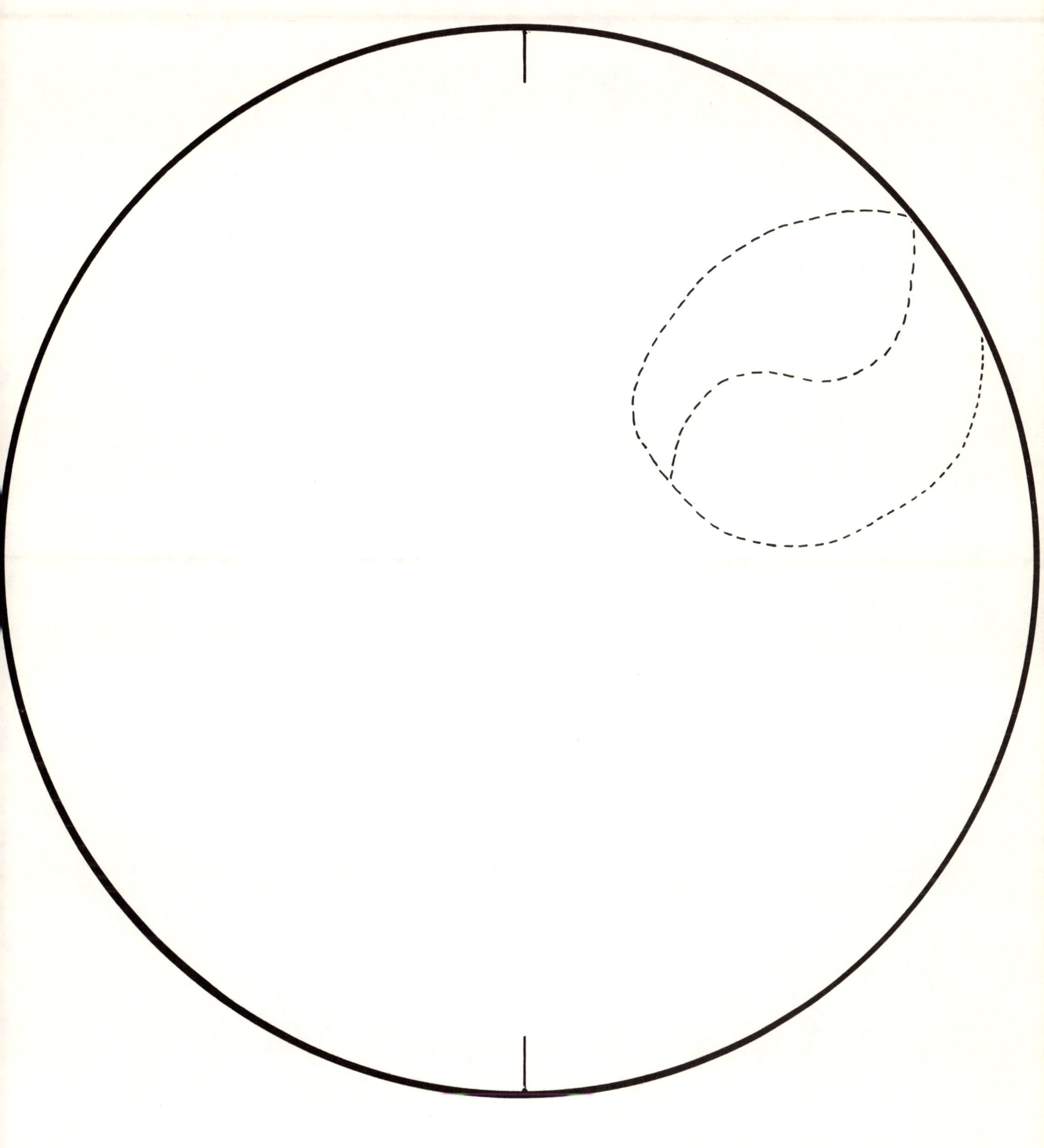

LITTLE BLACK CAT

LITTLE BLACK CAT

Little black cat **(1)**
On Halloween night
Sat on the fence
In the yellow moonlight. **(2)**

Black cat, black cat
What do you spy
Flying across
The Halloween sky?

I see two ghosts **(3)**
Floating by
Doing somersaults
In the sky.

Black cat, black cat
What else do you spy
Flying across
The Halloween sky? **(4)**

I see a black bat **(5)**
Flying by **(6)**
The big yellow moon
Up in the sky.

CUTTING DIRECTIONS

(1) Cut out the cat.

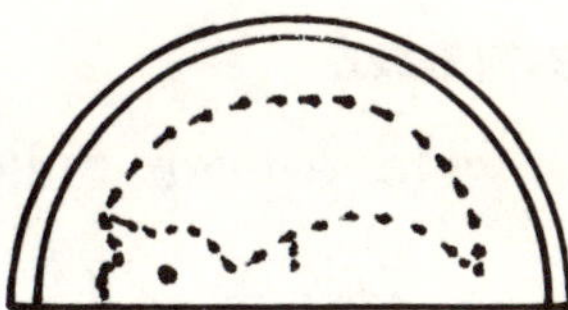

(2) Draw or punch out eyes on cat and hold up.

(3) Draw or punch out eyes for ghosts and hold up.

(4) Cut slits on side of ghosts and on the side of cat as shown.

(5) Slide the back of the ghosts into the sides of the cat, making a flying bat.

(6) Move the moon up and down, so that the bat will flap its wings.

EXTENDED ACTIVITIES

Movement

Have your children act out the following rhyme.

Black cat, black cat
Turn around.
Black cat, black cat
Touch the ground.

Black cat, black cat
Jump up high.
Black cat, black cat
Touch the sky.

Black cat, black cat
Bend down low.
Black cat, black cat
Touch your toe.

Black bat, black bat
Fly around
Black bat, black bat
Touch the ground.

Black bat, black bat
Fly up high
Black bat, black bat
Touch the sky.

Black bat, black bat
Fly down low.
Black bat, black bat
Touch my toe.

Music

HAVE YOU EVER SEEN A BLACK CAT?

Sung to: "Have You Ever Seen A Lassie?"

Have you ever seen a black cat,
A black cat, a black cat
Have you ever seen a black cat
That rides on a broom?

He zooms, and zooms, and zooms, and zooms.
Have you ever seen a black cat,
That rides on a broom?

Have you ever seen a black bat,
A black bat, a black bat
Have you ever seen a black bat
That flys past the moon?

The moon, the moon, the moon, the moon
Have you ever seen a black bat,
That flys past the moon?

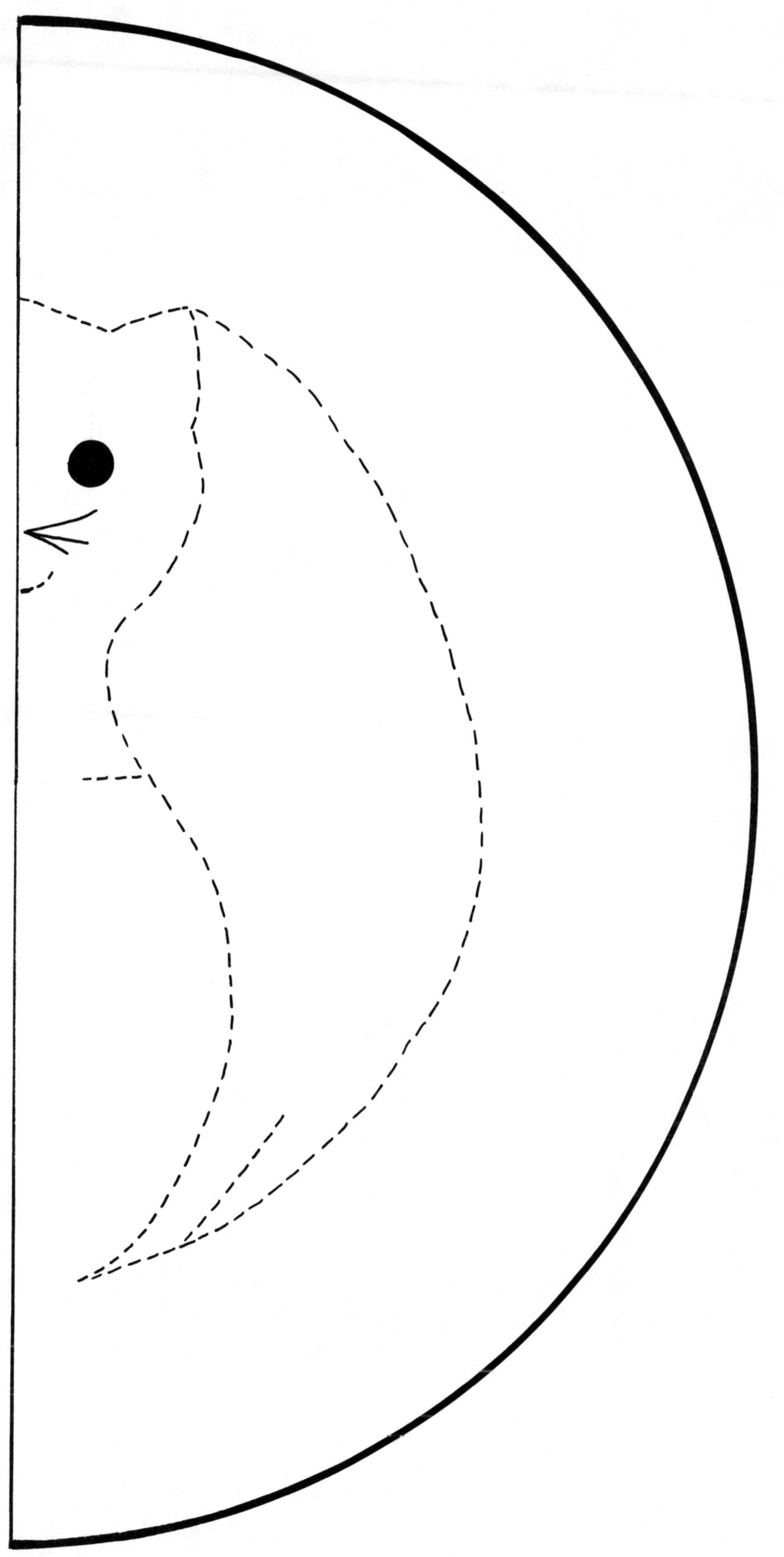

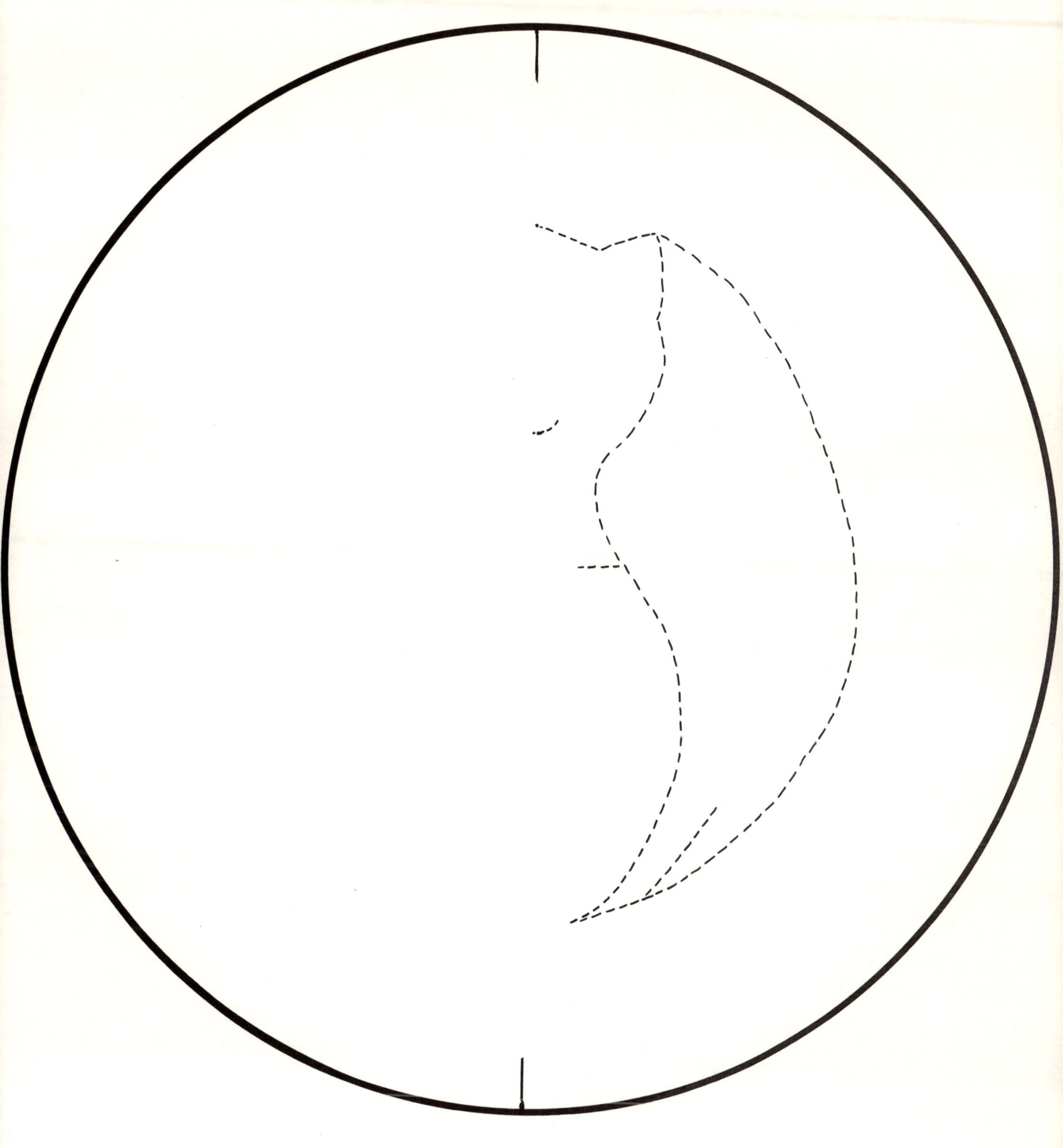

TWO FRIENDLY GHOSTS

TWO FRIENDLY GHOSTS

Once upon a time, there were two friendly ghosts named Happy and Glad. **(1) (2)**

Since they were happy all of the time, they wanted everyone to be happy. They spent most of their days doing good deeds, helping others.

One Halloween, while they were out helping children to cross the streets, they saw a little witch sitting on the curb crying.
"What's wrong Little Witch," they asked. "Can we help make you happy?"
"Boo, hoo," cried Little Witch. "It's Halloween and I've lost my broom. I'll miss all the fun if I can't fly through the sky."

Happy and Glad flew all over the town looking for the Little Witch's broom, but they couldn't find it. At last, they had an idea. They flew off and when they came back, they brought a large hot air balloon. **(3) (4)**

"Here Little Witch, now you can fly around on Halloween and you won't miss any of the fun."

Little Witch was happy again and so were Happy and Glad.

Off rode Little Witch.

And they heard her sing — as she flew past the moon

"Up, Up and away — On my beautiful balloon."

CUTTING DIRECTIONS

(1) Cut out ghosts.

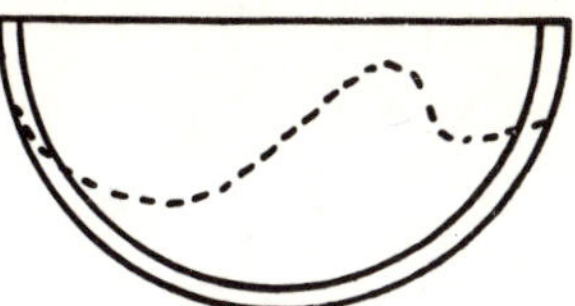

(2) Show two ghosts. Draw on faces if you wish.

(3) Open up the balloon.

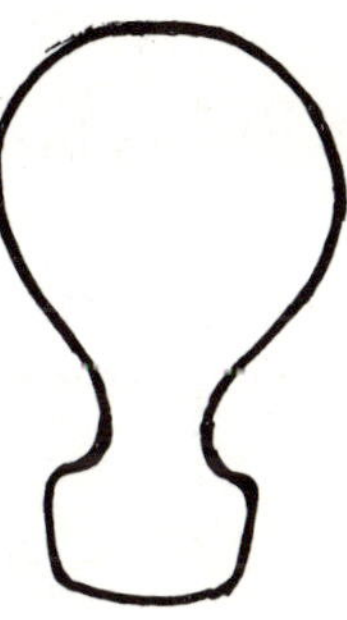

(4) Decorate the balloon with basket lines on the bottom basket and a design on the balloon.

EXTENDED ACTIVITIES

Art Activities

Ghost Pictures—

Materials: White paper, white crayon, paint brushes, black paint.

Procedure: Draw ghosts on white paper with a white crayon.

Activity: Have your children paint across the paper with thin black paint. Ghosts will appear like magic!

Ghost Puppets—

Materials: Soft white paper towels or white cotton material, black marking pen, cardboard.

Procedure: Make a pattern for a simple hand puppet. Cut out a double thickness of the puppet shape from an old sheet or else use two soft white paper towels. Sew around the edges of the puppet, leaving the bottom open.

Activity: Let your child draw a spooky face on their ghost with a black marking pen. (To prevent marking pen from soaking through to the back of the puppet, slide a piece of cardboard inside the puppet before the children start drawing.)

The nice thing about this activity is that there are no right or wrong ghost faces. Whatever the child draws is correct.

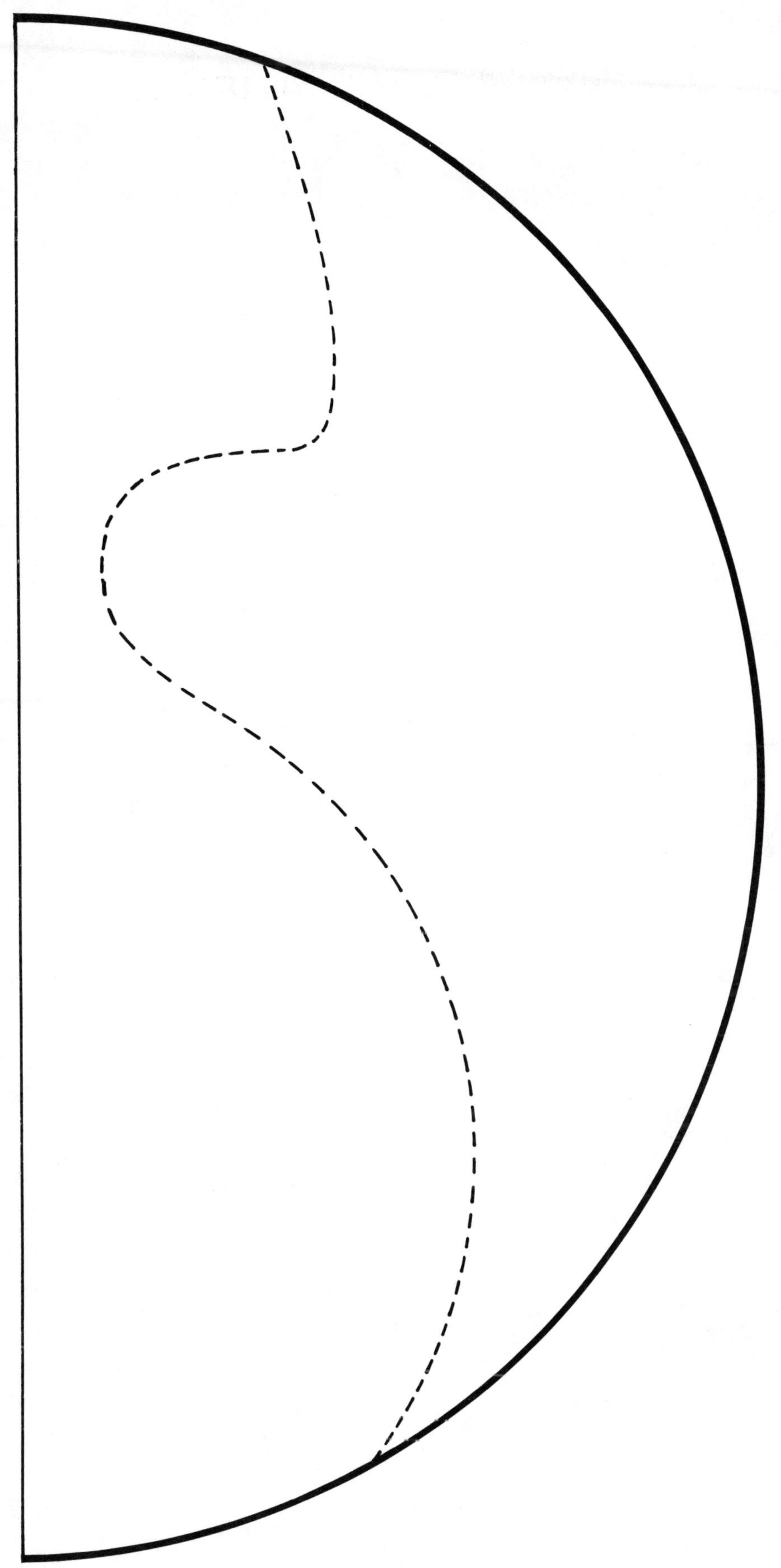

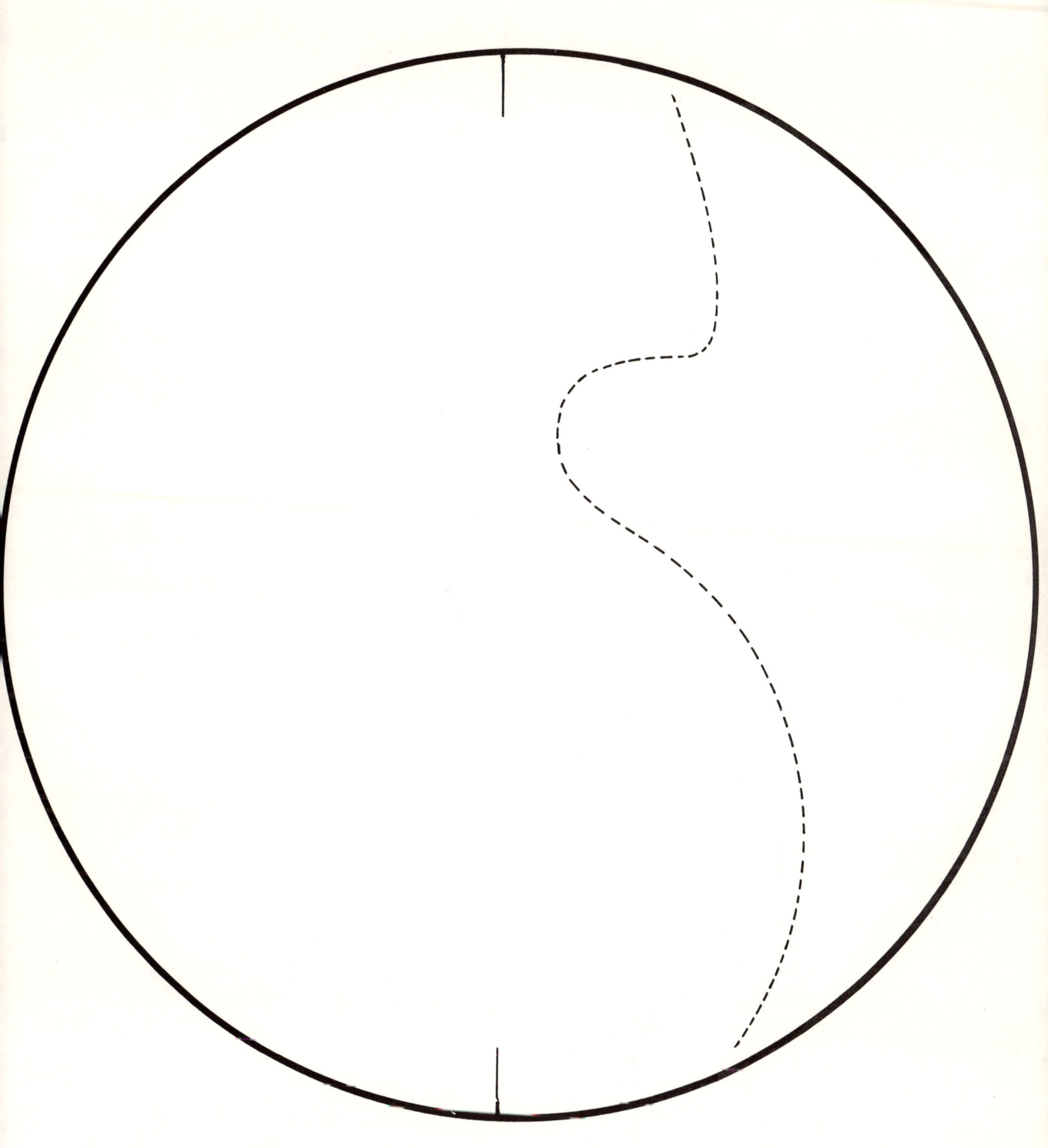

THREE BRAVE HUNTERS

THREE BRAVE HUNTERS

Three brave hunters
Set out one day
To capture a monster
Who lived far away. **(1)**

They rode their canoe **(2)**
Far, far from home
Till they came to the land
Where the monsters roam. **(3)**

They set up their tents **(4)**
Then looked around
For monster footprints
But none were found.

Just as they were getting
Ready for bed
Into their tent
Rolled a great big head. **(5)**

It's eyes were aglow
It's face wore a grin
And when it opened its mouth
They saw fire within.

The hunters grabbed their things
And ran away
Back to their homes
Where they planned to stay.

They didn't hear the monster
Ask if they could play!
And they didn't see him cry
As they ran away.

CUTTING DIRECTIONS

(1) Cut out canoe.

(2) Hold up the canoe.

(3) Cut out the triangles.

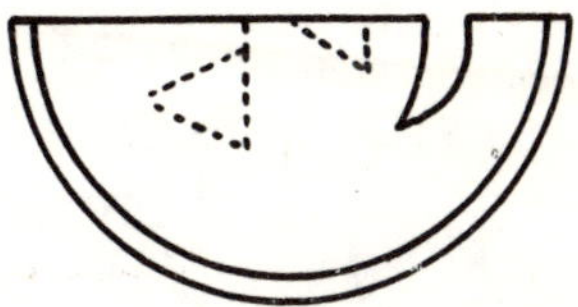

(4) Hold up the three tents.

(5) Hold up the jack-o-lantern.

EXTENDED ACTIVITIES

Dramatics

Re-read the story and have your children act out the story using hand and body movements.

Examples:

Hunting (hand held on over brow)
Rowing (rowing motions with hands)
Pitching tents (pretend to put up tents)
Surprise and fear when they see the pumpkin.
Rowing home.

Feelings

Use the story to introduce a discussion on feelings.

Ask questions, such as:

Was there really a monster in the story?
Why was the jack-o-lantern sad?
Why did the hunters think he was a monster?
What would you do if a jack-o-lantern rolled into your room?

Music

The story can be sung to the tune of "Frere Jacques" or "Mary Had A Little Lamb."

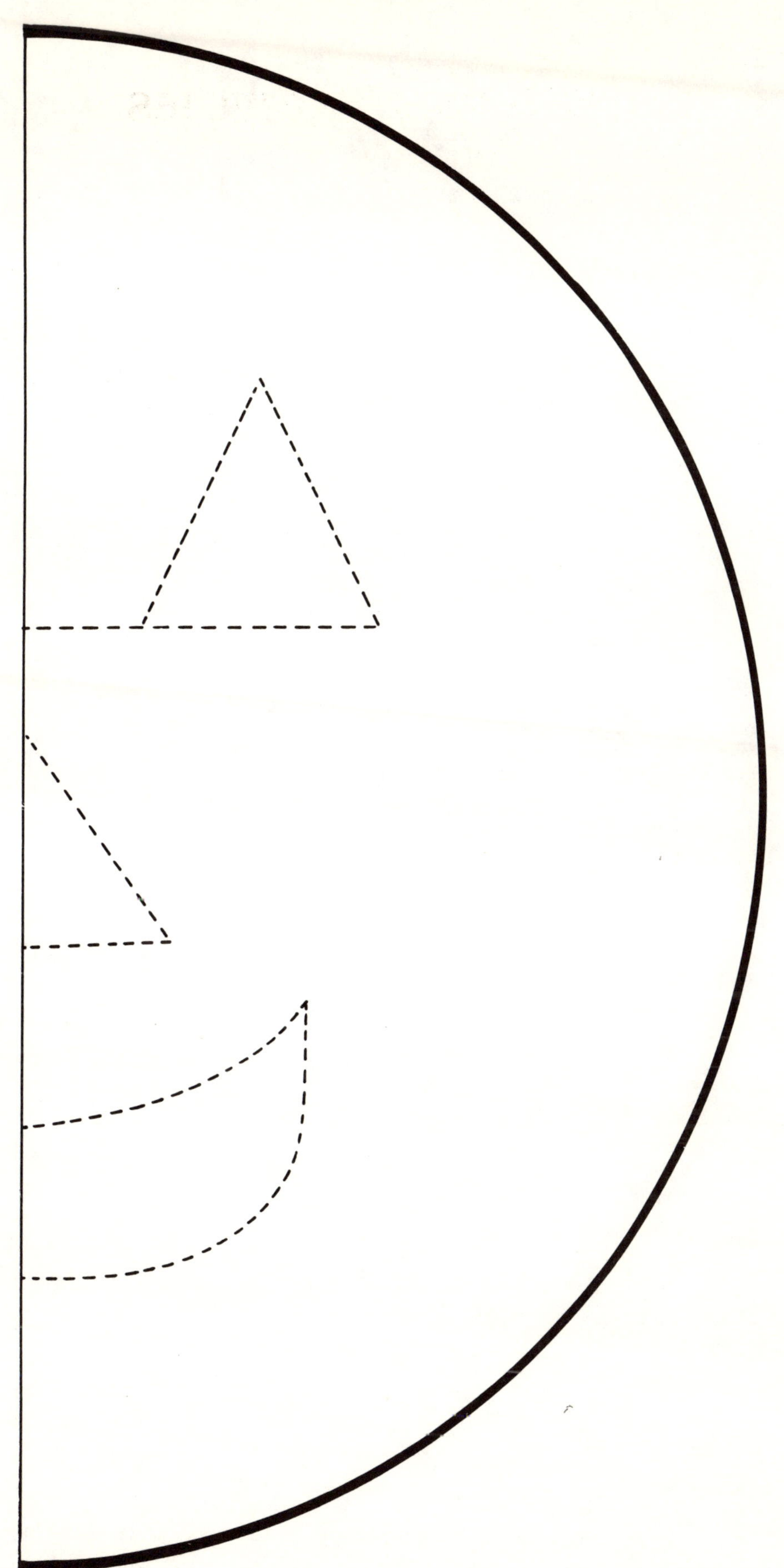

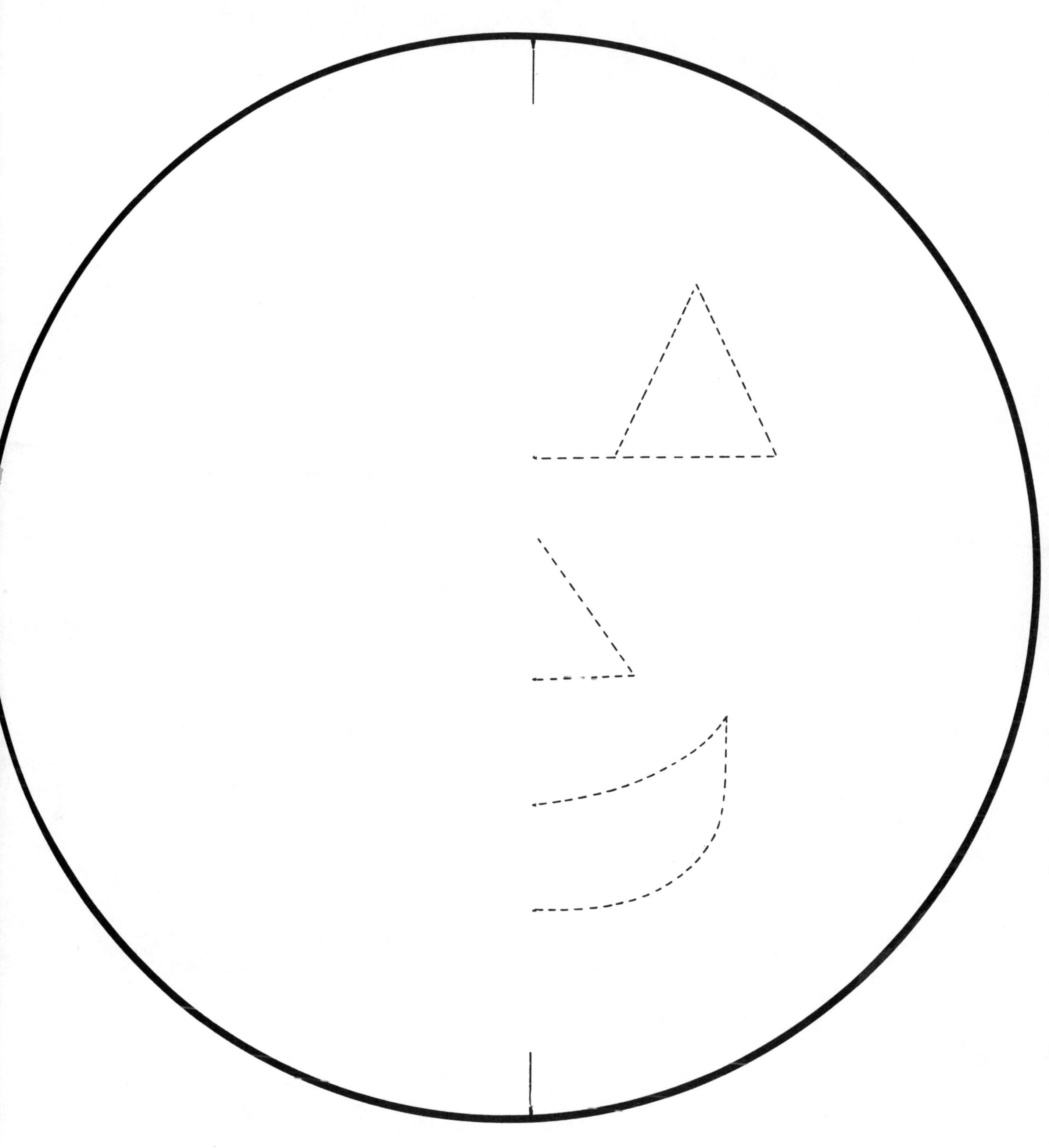

THE WISE OLD OWL

THE WISE OLD OWL

Adapted from an Indian folktale

Once upon a time, there were two little mice who lived in a big old farm house. **(1) (2)**

The farmer didn't mind having the mice around but the farmer's wife said they made too much mess and she wanted to get rid of them. **(3)**

So she went to the wise old owl and asked him what she could do. "Simple," said the owl, "get a cat." So the farmer's wife brought home a cat. Soon the mice were gone but the cat often broke things when it jumped up on the furniture. This made the wife mad so she went back to the wise old owl.

"Please, Mr. Owl, how can I get rid of the cat?" "Simple," said the owl, "get a dog." So the woman got a dog and took it home. Soon the cat was gone but the woman wasn't happy. The dog barked too much and chewed up her slippers. Back went the woman to the owl.

"Mr. Owl, please tell me how I can get rid of the dog." "Simple," said the owl, "get a tiger." So the farmer's wife bought a tiger and took it home. The dog left quickly, but much to her dismay, the woman watched the tiger run through her house smashing everything in sight.

Back went the woman to the owl. "Mr. Owl, please tell me how I can get rid of a tiger?" "Simple," said the wise old owl, "get an elephant." Off the woman went to buy an elephant and took it home. When the tiger saw the elephant, he left in a hurry. But the woman watched in horror as the elephant broke windows and put holes through walls. "Oh, no," cried the woman, "what can I do?"

So back she went to the owl. "Please, Mr. Owl, tell me how I can get rid of an elephant. "Simple," said the owl, "get two small mice!"

So the woman went in search of two small mice and took them home. **(4)**

When the elephant saw the mice he ran quickly out of the house. And the farmer and his wife and the two mice lived happily ever after in the big old farm house.

CUTTING DIRECTIONS

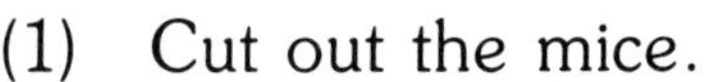

(1) Cut out the mice.

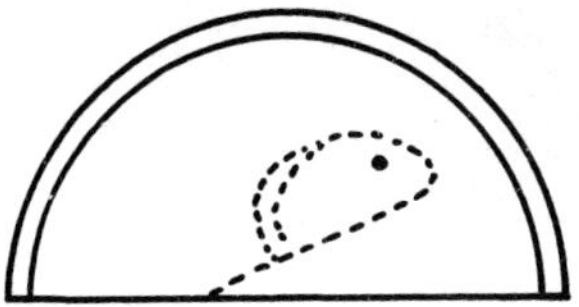

(2) Hold up the mice.

(3) Open up the plate to reveal an owl.

(4) Hold up mice again.

EXTENDED ACTIVITIES

Dramatics

Let your children act out the story, taking turns being the owl, the farmer and his wife and the other animals.

Music

WISE OLD OWL

Sung to: "Mary Had A Little Lamb"

Wise old owl up in the tree,
In the tree, in the tree.
Wise old owl up in the tree,
Will you come and __________ with me.

Let your children choose an activity to do with the owl and then let them sing about it as they do the movements.

Examples of actions children could sing about:

Sing	Run
Dance	Fly
Skip	Spin
Jump	Hop

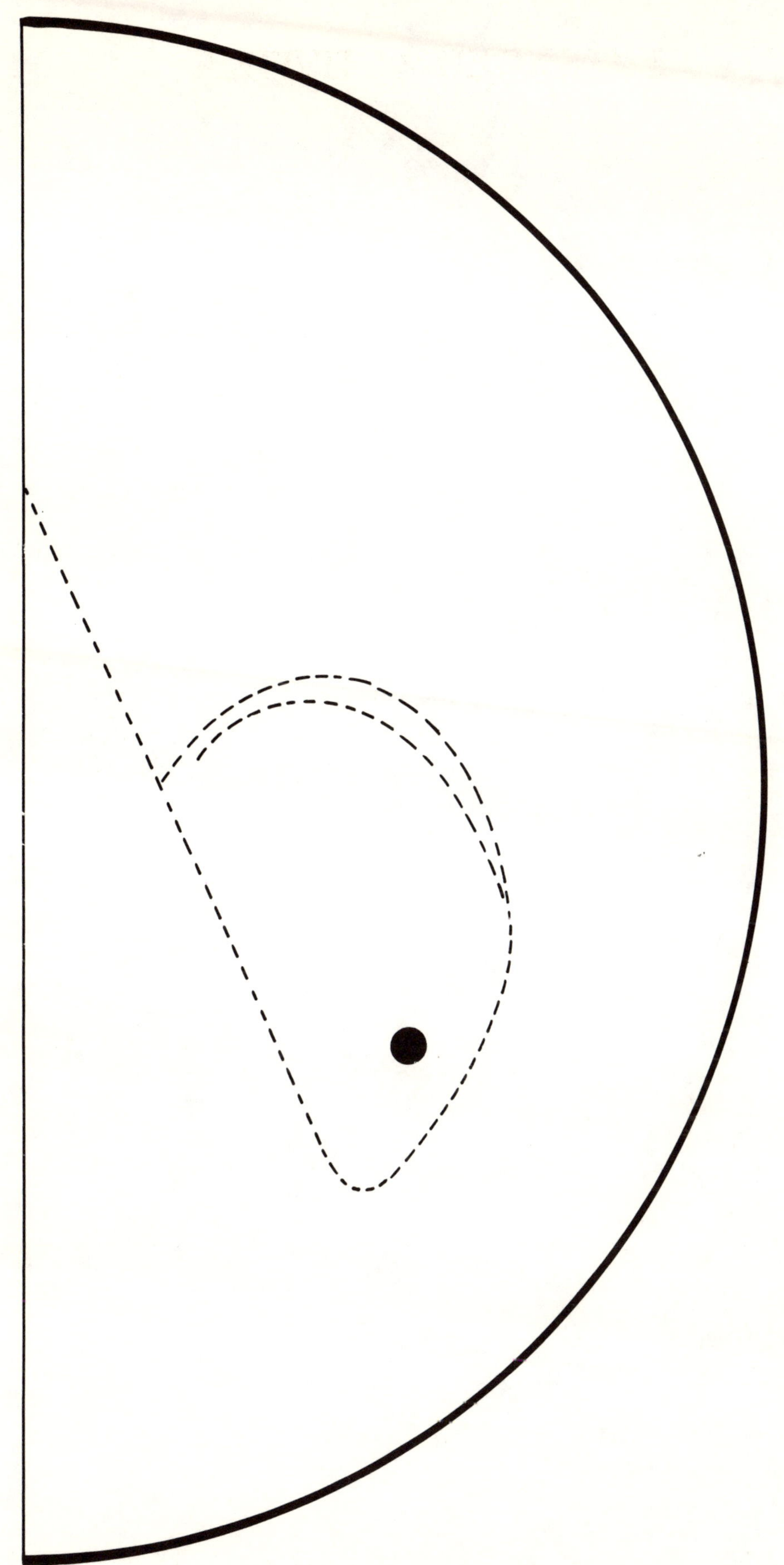

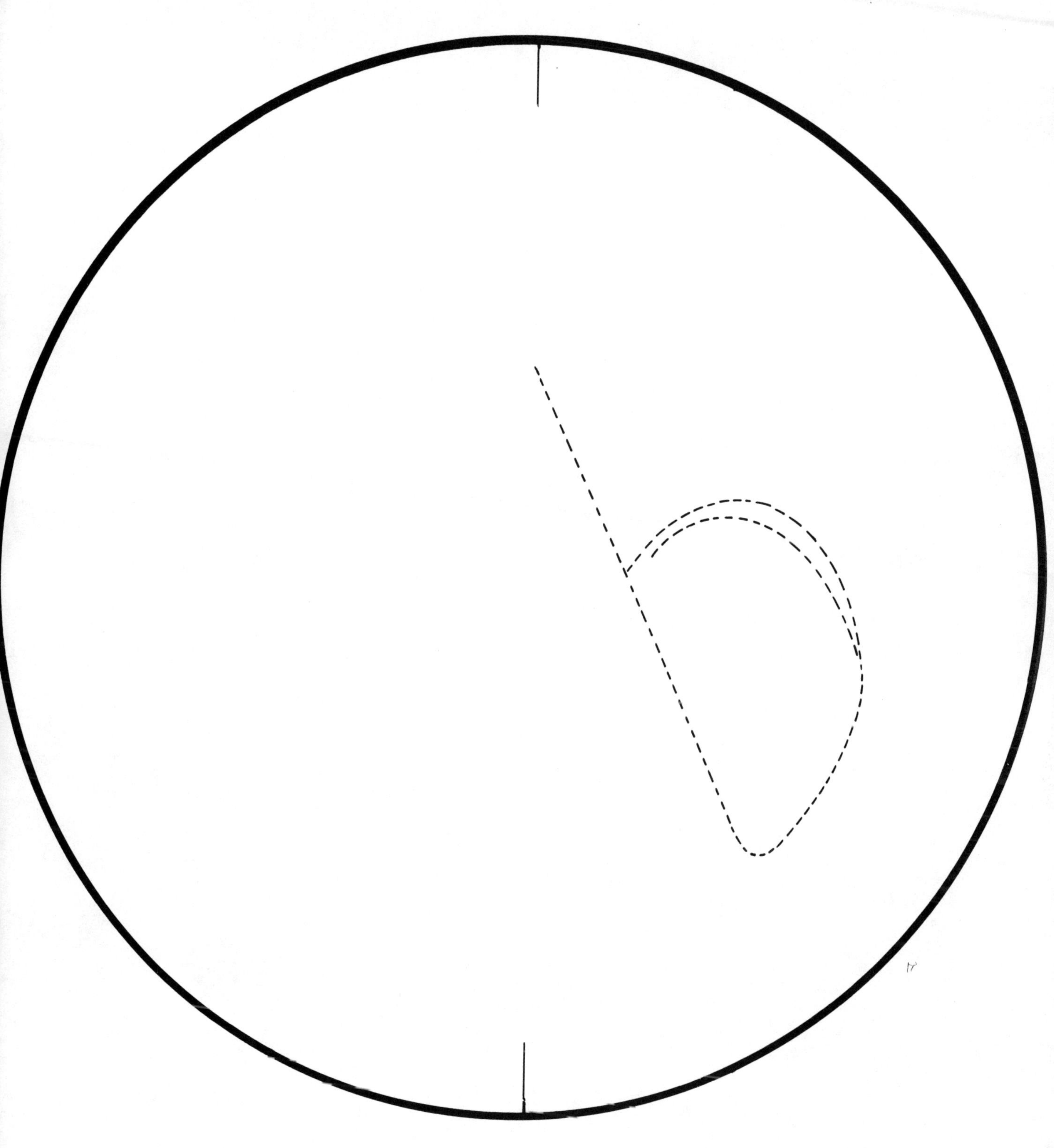

LITTLE TURKEY

LITTLE TURKEY

(1) (2) (3) (4) (5) (6)
Little turkey sat in the barn all day
Wishing that he could go out and play.

But not till he was bigger — till he was full grown
Could little turkey play in the yard all alone.

Little turkey wished and what do you know
Little turkey wished and started to grow.

Out puffed his tummy to a great big size **(7)**
Out from his tail — a big surprise! **(8)**

Now little turkey was all full grown
Now little turkey could go out alone.

CUTTING DIRECTIONS

(1) Fold a paper plate in half.

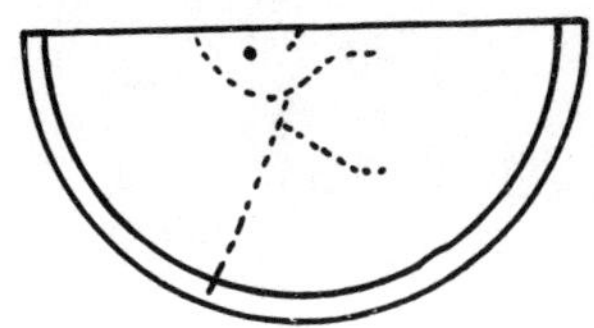

(2) Cut along cutting lines. Use hole to make eyes or draw them on.

(3) Fold back middle flaps and head.

(4) Roll larger flaps towards the middle. Hold in place with your fingers.

(5) Fold back head and small flaps.

(6) Lay turkey down, push head back. Cut-out should resemble a small turkey.

(7) Open turkey back out flat. Fold flaps backwards around behind the turkey. Hook back of turkey together with slits (directions page 77). Fold wings down.

(8) Stick the remaining section from the plate down behind the turkey's head, hooking it down in the side wing slits. Voila! Spread tail feathers!

EXTENDED ACTIVITIES

Music

HA HA TURKEY IN THE STRAW

Sung to: "Skip To My Lou"

Turkey in the brown straw, ha ha ha
Turkey in the brown straw, ha ha ha
Turkey in the brown straw, ha ha ha
Skip to My Lou My Darling.

Ha Ha, turkey in the straw
Ha Ha, turkey in the straw
Ha Ha, turkey in the straw
Turkey in the straw, My Darling.

Continue singing with such verses as:

Turkey in the white snow, ho ho ho
or
Turkey in the blue sky, hi hi hi
or
Turkey in the yellow corn, horn, horn, horn
or
Turkey in the green tree, he he he
or
Turkey in the red hay, hay hay hay

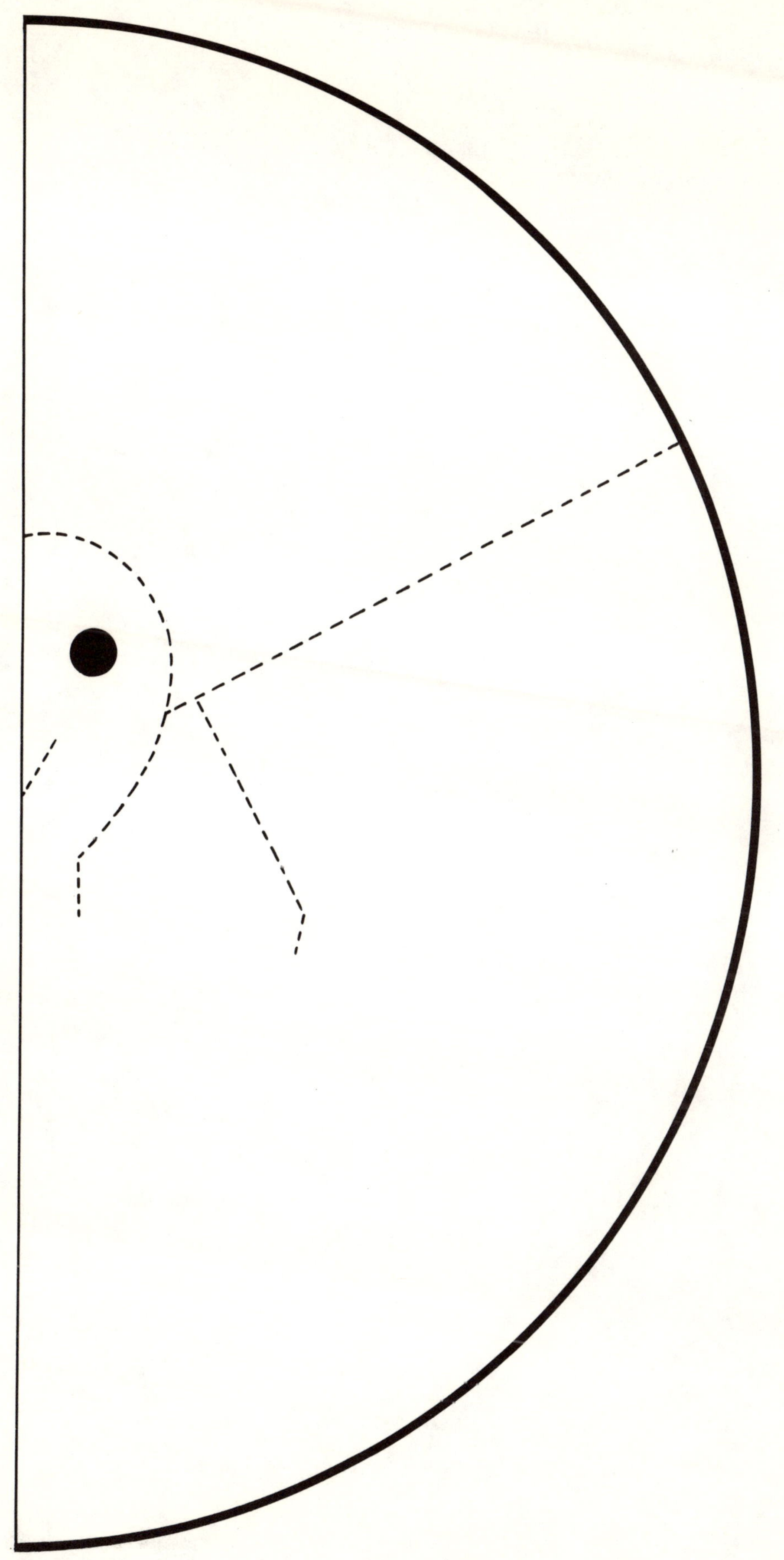

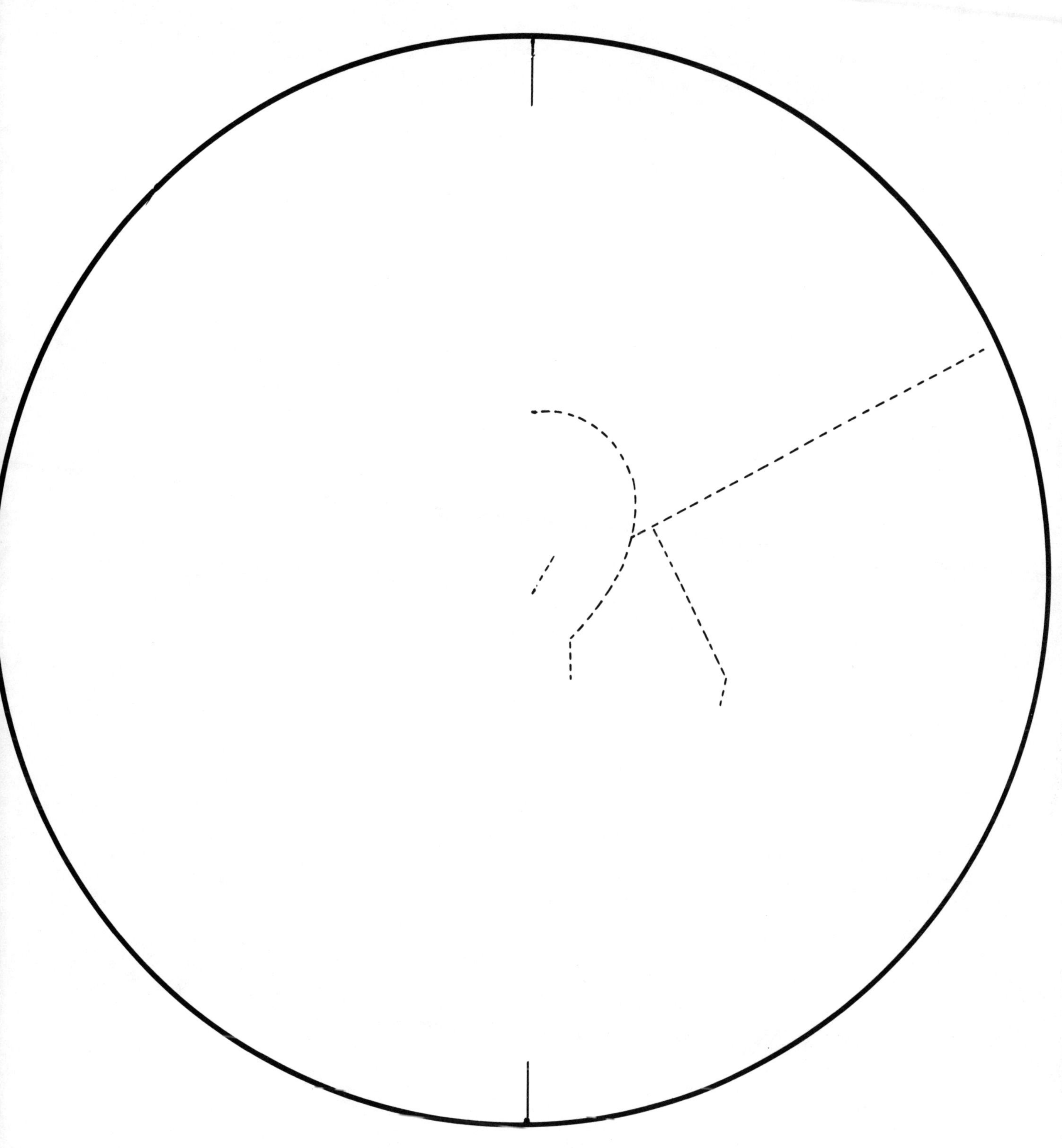

BACK HOOK-UPS

Below are directions for hooking two sides together so that a cut-out can stand up on its own.

Bring the two pieces together. Cut one side down from the top halfway. Cut the other side up from the bottom halfway.

Now slide the side cut from the bottom — down onto the top slit on the other side, hooking the two sides together.

Sometimes it works best to cut the slits at a slight angle as shown.

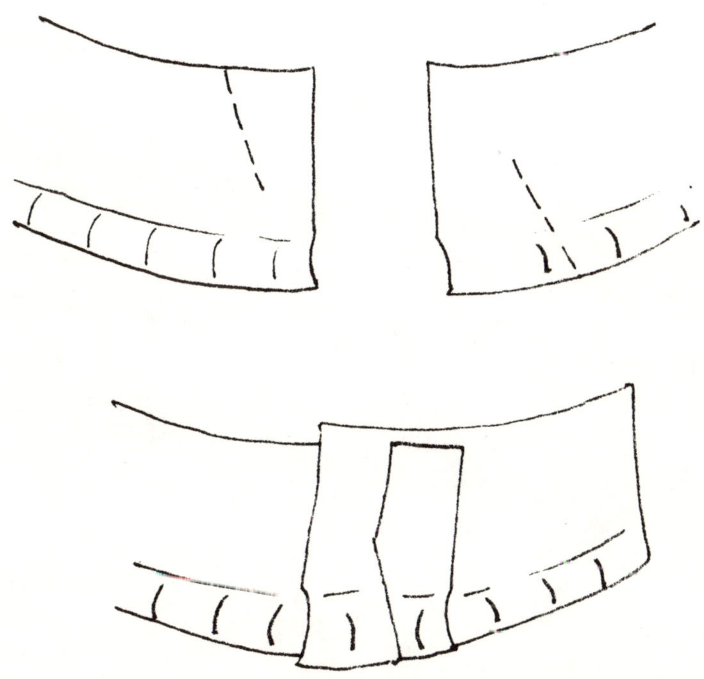

TOTLINE PRESS

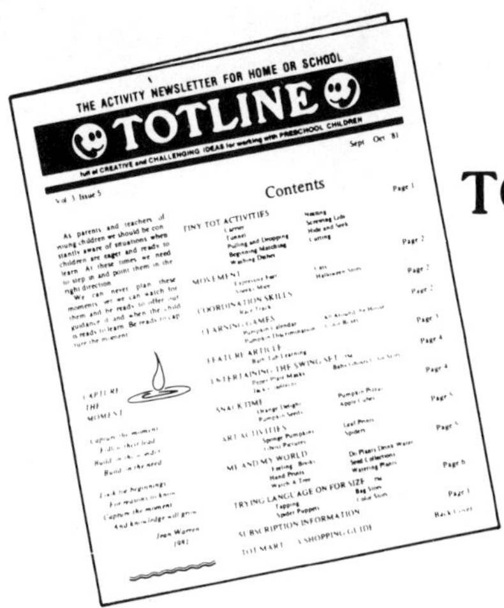

TOTLINE NEWSLETTER **$12/yr. (6 issues)**

24 pages full of ideas for working with preschool children. Written by: Jean Warren. The "Totline" features activities in art, creative movement, coordination, learning games, party ideas, music, science, self-awareness, sugarless snacks, language activities, original stories, feature articles and a special infant-toddler page.

SUPER SNACKS **$3.95 64 pg. softcover**

The seasonal snack book that uses no sugar, honey or artificial sweeteners. Written by: Jean Warren. 160 recipes full of delicious alternatives to help break the "cupcake/koolaid" habit. The recipes are taken from back issues of the Totline newsletter.

PIGGYBACK SONGS **$4.95 64 pg. softcover**

MORE PIGGYBACK SONGS **$6.95 96 pg. softcover**

Each book contains new songs sung to the tunes of childhood favorites. The songs are easy for both children and adults to learn because you already know the tunes. Each book contains original songs for holiday and special times during the year, plus general songs young children will enjoy. The original "Piggyback Songs" book contains 110 songs and the sequel book "More Piggyback Songs" contains 196 new songs. Both books are chorded for guitar and autoharp.

Books available from:

Totline Press P.O. Box 2255 Everett, WA 98203

Include 10% for postage and handling • U.S. Funds only • WA state orders include 7.8% sales tax

ADDITIONAL BOOKS BY JEAN WARREN

CRAFTS
$6.95 80 pg. softbound

A collection of seasonal craft activities for working with young children. The ideas are easy, fun and inexpensive. Written by Jean Warren and compiled from back issues of the Totline newsletter. *Ages 3-8*

LEARNING GAMES
$6.95 80 pg. softbound

A collection of over 100 learning games you can make for teaching concepts, such as: color, number, size, shape, etc. to young children. The ideas are easy, fun and inexpensive. Written by Jean Warren and taken from back issues of the Totline newsletter. *Ages 3-6*

LANGUAGE GAMES
$6.95 80 pg. softbound

A collection of 100 unstructured language activities to encourage language development in young children. The ideas are easy, fun and inexpensive. Written by Jean Warren and taken from back issues of the Totline newsletter. *Ages 4-6*

MOVEMENT TIME
$6.95 80 pg. softbound

A seasonal collection of open-ended movement activities for young children. Written by Jean Warren. Taken from back issues of the Totline newsletter. *Ages 3-8*

SCIENCE TIME
$6.95 80 pg. softbound

A seasonal collection of science activities for young children. Fun for both adults and children. Written by Jean Warren. Taken from back issues of the Totline newsletter. *Ages 3-8*

STORY TIME
$6.95 80 pg. softbound

A delightful collection of open-ended language experiences. The book includes creative stories, rhymes and songs which the child helps to create. Written by Jean Warren and taken from back issues of the Totline newsletter. *Ages 3-8*

The above books are from the
MONDAY MORNING Play & Learn Series
available from:

Totline Press P.O. Box 2255 Everett, WA 98203

Add 10% for postage & handling • U.S. Funds only • WA state orders add 7.8% tax